10/96

NOV 1997
5^{00}
1x

25X
———
7/10

D0050826

1-2 CR

CHICAGO AND THE CAT

The Family Reunion

WRITTEN AND ILLUSTRATED BY

Robin Michal Koontz

A LITTLE CHAPTER BOOK

COBBLEHILL BOOKS/DUTTON • NEW YORK

This book is for the Denmarks & the Germers and all their kin.
Special thanks to Jim, the Norwegian Moose.

Library of Congress Cataloging-in-Publication Data
Koontz, Robin Michal.
Chicago and the cat : the family reunion /
written and illustrated by Robin Michal Koontz.
p.   cm.
Summary: Chicago the rabbit and her friend the cat
host a reunion of Rabbit's very large family.
ISBN 0-525-65202-7 (hardcover)
[1. Rabbits—Fiction.   2. Cats—Fiction.
3. Family reunions—Fiction.]   I. Title.
PZ7.K83574Ck   1996   [E]—dc20   95-12734   CIP   AC
Published in the United States by Cobblehill Books,
an affiliate of Dutton Children's Books,
a division of Penguin Books USA Inc.,
375 Hudson Street, New York, New York 10014
Typography by Kathleen Westray
Printed in Hong Kong   First Edition
10 9 8 7 6 5 4 3 2 1

CHAPTER 1: THE PLAN

"Hey, cat!" cried Chicago.

"Shush!" said the cat.

"You'll scare the birds away."

"You leave those birds alone," said Chicago.

"I was just looking at them," said the cat.

"What's up?"

Chicago waved a letter in the cat's face.

"My Aunt Philly and Uncle Denver
are coming to visit," she said.

"And they want to have a family reunion!"

"HERE?" cried the cat.

"How many rabbits are in your family?"

"A bunch," said Chicago.

"Oh, no," groaned the cat.

"Where will we put them all?"

"We have lots of room," said Chicago.

"What will we feed them all?" asked the cat.

"That's the best part," said Chicago.

"My family will bring the food!"

"Oboy!" said the cat.

Chicago ran into the house
to write the invitations.

"I wonder how many rabbits
are in a bunch," said the cat.

"Hey, cat," said Chicago.

"This is Aunt Philly and Uncle Denver!"

Aunt Philly grabbed the cat

and kissed her face.

"Ack!" cried the cat.

"Hey, cat!" cried Uncle Denver.

"Give me a hand with this food, will you?"

"Glad to," said the cat.

She grabbed a box.

"What is that terrible smell?" asked the cat.

"Carrotburger mix," said Uncle Denver.

"Whatburger?" asked the cat.

"Or maybe it's spinach dogs," said Uncle Denver.

"Spinach dogs!" cried the cat.

"Ah, you must smell the dandelion casserole with brussels sprouts," said Uncle Denver. "It's one of my favorites."

"I'm going to throw up," mumbled the cat.

"Didn't you bring any real food?" she asked.

"Try one of these," said Uncle Denver.
He handed the cat a green lollipop.
"What is it?" asked the cat.
"Zucchini Pop," said Uncle Denver.

"Thanks, but no thanks," she said.
"I think I'll stick with tuna fish."
"You don't know what's good,"
mumbled Uncle Denver.

CHAPTER 3: BEDTIME

"Time for bed, everyone!" said Chicago.

"No rabbits in my room, right?" asked the cat.

"Uh, oh," said Chicago.

"What do you mean 'uh, oh'?" asked the cat.

"We put a few kids in your room."

"Ack!" cried the cat.

"Oh, come on, cat," said Chicago.

"It's only for one night."

"Yes," said Aunt Philly.

"And besides, they're all sleeping."

"Oh, all right," said the cat.

She went to her room and turned on the light.

Her room was filled with rabbits.

"Hiya, cat!"

"Oh my gosh," said the cat.

"This is just a few kids?"

"We're having a slumber party!"

cried the rabbits.

"Come and play with us!"

"I thought you were supposed
to be sleeping," said the cat.
"No sleeping!" cried the rabbits.
They began to jump up and down
on the cat's bed.
"Hey!" yelled the cat.
"You kids go to sleep right now!"
"No!" cried the rabbits.

"No?" asked the cat.

The rabbits swung on the closet door.
"You have to make us!" they cried.

The rabbits began tossing things out
of the cat's drawers.
"How?" cried the cat.

"You have to promise
to do something," they said.

"What? I'll do anything!" cried the cat.

"Be our umpire at the family baseball game."

"Is that all?" asked the cat.

"Yup," said the rabbits.

"Okay!" agreed the cat.

"Now go to sleep, please!"

"Oboy!" said the rabbits.

The cat turned off the light.

CHAPTER 4: THE PICNIC

"What a beautiful day
for a reunion," said Chicago.
"What's so great about it?"
grumbled the cat.

"What's the matter?" asked Chicago.

"I didn't get much sleep," said the cat.

"Don't be a grump-lip," said Chicago.

"Here, cat, have a spinach dog!"

Splat! Aunt Philly slopped

a dog on the cat's plate.

"You will love my oatmeal salad."
Splush! Aunt Philly spooned a hunk
of brown stuff on the cat's plate.

"Here, try some fried lettuce!"
Blap! She splashed green goo
on the cat's plate.

"Yuk!" cried the cat.

"Where's the tuna fish?"

"Oops," said Chicago.

"We ran out."

The cat stared at her plate.

"That's okay," she said.

"I've lost my appetite."

CHAPTER 5: RABBITBALL

"Hey, everyone," cried Uncle Denver.

"Let's play ball!"

They headed to the baseball field.

Aunt Philly was up. Chicago pitched.
Swish!

"Strike one!" yelled the cat.

"No way," said Aunt Philly.

"It was right over the plate!" cried the cat.

Aunt Philly moved the plate.

"Was not," she said.

She smiled at the cat.

"Ball one," sighed the cat.

Chicago pitched the ball again.

Crack! Aunt Philly ran.

"Foul ball!" cried the cat.

"Not!" cried Aunt Philly,
as she rounded the bases.

"It went into the bleachers!" cried the cat.

"But I threw it back," said Uncle Denver.

The cat scratched her head.

"Just what kind

of baseball is this?" she asked.

"Rabbitball!" cried the rabbits.

"I should have known," mumbled the cat.

Uncle Denver stepped to the plate.

"Give me a fast ball, Chicago," he said.

The ball flew past Uncle Denver.

CRACCCCKKKKKK!

Lightning lit up the sky.

Uncle Denver ran.

"Home run?" asked the cat.

"GAME!" cried Chicago.

They all ran into the house.

"We need an inside project," said Chicago.
"Any ideas?"
"Sure," said the cat.
"Let's build a bird feeder."

CHAPTER 6: GOOD-BYE

"There they go," said Chicago.

"Thank goodness!" said the cat.

"Tell the truth, cat," said Chicago.

"You had a good time, right?"

"The bird feeder turned
out great," said the cat.
"You, cat, you," said Chicago.
"I can't wait until
the next reunion," said the cat.

"You mean you want to
   do this again?" asked Chicago.
"You bet!" said the cat.
"Only next time, it will be MY family."
"Uh, oh," said Chicago.

"How many cats are we talking about?"
"Heh, heh," chuckled the cat.
"A bunch."